DIASPORADIC:

The Collected Thought Processes of a Hyphenated-American

by Zaki

PublishAmerica
Baltimore

First printing

At the specific preference of the author, PublishAmerica allowed this work to remain exactly as the author intended, verbatim, without editorial input.

ISBN: 1-4241-2208-2
PUBLISHED BY PUBLISHAMERICA, LLLP
www.publishamerica.com
Baltimore

Printed in the United States of America

Dedication

This collection is dedicated to the eternal Light of infinite wisdom which connects me to, and guides me through on my quest for a greater understanding of my place within the vast African Diaspora.
Also to my future, Zamani, Khairi and Zuhri.

Acknowledgments

I would like to thank the Creator for every morning, and my mother and father for every lesson. Love to my wisdom, Amira, for all those things which words cannot explain. Peace to my sisters and brothers, Janese, Rhodda, Ursula, James, Joe and Tarris, for loving me anyway. I also have to thank the rest of my family (Bell, Bowers and Woodall) for keeping my foundation solid. Peace to hip hop for the umbrella, especially Luther Campbell (2 Live Crew), N.W.A. and Wu-Tang.

Table of Conscience

linear motion

my time is not lost, spent
or subjected...perfected in my mind,
it will not stand the test of encapsulation...
no constraints to be placed...
i cannot lay it to waste...or travel
back into it...though so many have misconstrued it,
my time is not of the essence...
not classic
at any given period or moment...
i once believed i owned it...
force of reality
does not wane...even if i serve it,
i never regain pieces of my past...
i outlast by focus on my control panel...
warp speed is reached
when i invoke divine wisdom...it does not
wait for men...once i knew,
it would be all around me...engulfed in the sands,
mine does not become shorter...
perpetual drops of water provide the illusion of a measure...
circular motion does the same...
known to heal wounds,
its end has been the bane of my kind...
they want to draw a line from the unknown
to the unknown...without a wick
or a tick,
and still being blown out of proportion...
the distortion benefits few...
while many have none in their possession...

any indiscretion will reverberate
eternally without creating a ripple...
conservatives,
moderates and liberals
waste much within a system...bureaucracy,
the anti-me and mine...
many dream to change it from within,
have strong wills and minds...
once dipped into the trenches, it seems,
they never find the...

inner solicitation

fragmented,
life ended on a last second play,
environment of labor
for slave pay enhanced,
despite associations for advanced
and no longer colored people,
there are looks of surprise when i say we're not equal,
what manner,
what mode,
what chain of events makes you believe
i should be convinced,
under pretense of protection i have attended your battles,
slaughtered cattle remains
spread over White plains,
white names identify,
provide ownership proof,
fire on the roof cause trickle down burning,
discerning eyes watch
as the tide begins turning,
yearning for more prey, the-ism metamorphoses,
the corporate rendition changed the pen to
offices,
exhausted possibility of working from within,
exposed inconsistency evaluates the trend,
bend but won't break,
zealots enshrine fake advertised
divine bodies of knowledge,
body of evidence demonstrates divine shortage,
drawbridge always raised to
inhibit freedom passage,
appeals to striving minds contained in this message...

break time lines

raindrops fall, eloquent,
with delicate speech...
no sound, divine,
wise with global reach...
deep into the crevice
of a brain malfunction...
intense reparation
of pollutant deconstruction...
with properties that cleanse,
the magnitude unknown...
slave deterrent liquid
brought life to the throne...
reunite with the elements
which form into one...
social sway of the winds,
tempered by the sun...
shining armor cause a
shimmer, deliverance fails...
not all-powerful,
yet and still all hail...

a teacher

my mind and i raced along the
lonely path toward self-
righteousness, raced
through the 'hood, where everyone
deserves what they get...
we crashed into Black dreams,
and shattered them...we
destroyed unworthy futures, then took
precautions to ensure
there will be a blemish...we
scarred the present,
reiterated our contradictory past...
my mind and eye felt little
remorse, but staged a
formal exhibition to shield
the ruse...we dashed
the hopes of the hopeless without
losing focus...
timeless, soul-less, boldness identifies
the coldness—as darkness
descends upon the realm of my destruction...
my passion reserved for those
material symbols of my arrival...
induction into the hall
of shame, though i will not attend
the ceremony...survival
is my bottom line...and although
i left them
on their bottom,

lying in a pool of life force—death
became them...
and no one will do us part
just us for justice
just us for justice...

emancipated proclamation

i am unfinished business,
spiritually connected...divine intervention
leaves me protected...left to my
own devices, i concoct love potions...
pheromones from my dome
rub ashy brains like lotion...this notion,
when subjected to critical
observation, withstands all attempts
at invalidation...defenses
impenetrable...content to seek minimal
attention, i inspect formations
like army generals...
they're all out of regs., and unfit to serve...
honorably discharge them
when i spit these verbs...meaning i take
action, react to the false...
extrava-Danza, now they all know who's the
boss...
the man nanny, sent to raise up all the kids...
vocabulary Kunta,
mental graves, i dig...and
resurrect the souls and send them back to self...
bold predictions demonstrate
like chemistry sets...
unarmed resistance, overstand the
penalty is death...
unharmed in the trenches, not
an enemy left...
lay you down to sleep and pray your soul is

kept...
because i killed
my brother in this battle,
i wept...
i can't go on...

mile marker seven two

use of social norms to determine my fate,
lands my mind in a comatose state...
disease-filled,
with shrapnel from media, brain exposed...
in need of a surgeon,
state of depression imposed...supposed to be free,
but with new nomenclature...
can only detect nigga from designed self hatred...
made to follow a path of self-division,
with negative ideas as my personal prison...
i act out,
act bad,
act up,
but still act...
state of confusion about this energy i attract...
a fake, fact fiction was given as a gift...
Santa's little helpers,
the perpetrators of this great rift
in the function of my psyche...
now, a family liability...
a trivialized culture has become my new legacy...
from sage, mastered slave,
to bickering buffoon...
the spiritual divine element no longer
in tune with nature, or my own...
estranged from my mother...
the nutrients i have missed, as yet,
undiscovered...uncovered from
the murky depths in the state of a worm...
unleashed from the cocoon, a mass

of a deformed, deterred, digressed
vessel of detriment...passenger and co-pilot on
my journey through irrelevance...

men's room mania

eloquent speech is not
relevant...seek the element
which explains the event...
leading up to development of new strains
infectious mental strategies,
calibrated by analogies born of social reality,
not that in which status
maintenance is contingent...but that which
fosters cultural independence...
this dominance cannot sustain without ignorance...
can not complain,
and not contribute resistance...
bodies, minds trained for freedom
will insist this...simple matters eclipsed
by confusion, now reign...
elevated humanity seeks monetary gain...
voluntary manslaughter
mode of operation...designed to perpetuate
for the duration...spoken of as the
highest form of civilization...
depend upon oppressed zombies, division of labor...
destruction of hope,
faith and belief...replace with paper
champions, a powerful blow to the head...
head niggas in charge
in bed with the feds...killing the drive,
chop it off at the legs...
forever the down and distance
we dread...choose not to change possession,
go for it instead......

mind frame

a change in mind causes
a change in time...indicators of dissatisfaction
with carefully planned distractions...
turn back the hands of revolution,
as time moves forward,
onward,
upwards...of many million minions,
opinions spoken as fact...in
the act of justification for
random attacks on my legitimacy...infinitely
connected intimately, the melting pot
blood courses, despite high rate of divorces...
sources say
i'm on the brink of extinction...linking fate to present
condition...
move the debate out of the frying pan,
into the kitchen
where so many cannot stand the heat...
technique of enslavement
tried and true...
a view to the field has returned anew...
adjourn til able to produce a clue...
until i know what they all knew...

operating procedures

i'm obsessed with all these women who i don't trust,
them-due to a history of betrayal,
i lust them, living in denial
of my true potential
to love... whether entrenched
in a battle with the gods
over the nature
of this creature, or observing the sway of her
hips, my lips are sealed
until truth revealed... as i
kneel before the altar of the wise,
receiving guidance from the
Oracle of nature, my eyes play
tricks on my mind... behind
the shine and glitter should be
focused intervention... divine
attention given to details which
prevail in the end... need i mention the dynamic of original
sin???
as i begin to progress into
a regressive state,
the debate continues, leaving
only my future at stake... at this
rate i will exist only
in doubt, unable
to ascertain what all this is really about... no doubt, i will
remain intrigued; continue
to question... searching, not for
the answer, but for the instructions...

Seville Lee Ann

misinformed, expendable bystander, standing by. receiving
airwave intelligence. trying to decipher the relevance.
presuming protection from a threat. feeling threatened by
the protection. sensing domination motivation. historical
evidence adds to the equation. colorful persuasion bearing
the brunt of destruction. airwaves defining my function.
leading me against me. aspire to remove the veil intensely.
running out of time. a particular trick of the trade. dead
along the lines of loss. decision makers have say, but not pay
in the cost. heat in the region which is not the home. battle
takes on a face of its own. one chance, may have already
blown...

merry made

enter the garden, splendid in design...
mine for the taking,
shaking in my cool demeanor...
obscene dreamer when you are on tap,
on your back
or on your knees...
please, may i have you tonight,
as i fight back the urge
to splurge too soon...
still desire to enter your moon...
your body croons, sings the
pheromone song...
and although i am long,
you contain me, strong,
moist, soft and sweet taste...
laid to waste once i enter your place...
look on my face
denotes pure ecstasy...
remain inside while you stay lying
next to me...sex could be this,
but this is much more...
i attain bliss
when you open the door...
allow me to score,
take my best shot,
pop the kitty, dig deep...
reap the benefit of
your body, replete with living essence...
dresses,

skirts,
panties,
doors to your love pantry...
allowed to be handy,
your man of the hour,
i shower your body with kisses...
hits and misses,
and best regards...
you are so soft,
i am so hard...

the patient

once unleashed, this flood of sensual acrobatics
has us communicating in body
language...i undress you with my eyes,
and your hands follow these commands...
slowly, the subject of this
intercourse, the object of my desire is revealed...
physical specimen of perfection, hand-crafted
by the goddess of passion...my eyes do not deceive,
yet disbelief tames the anxiety
initiated by this revelation...tamed indeed
by the architectural design of
flawless curves; lips to hips,
body reacts to mind, receiving the message
clear over the pound of heartbeats...
the first touch, a gentle stroke; strength
in my hands weakened by
the softness of your skin...simultaneously
hardened as i caress you,
seduction calms as we proceed to divine
ecstasy...much to your pleasure, i speak
in tongue...religiously tasting
the candy that receives a
constant supply of sweetness from your
sugar walls...
kid in a candy store, voracious appetite for
spawning climactic episodes...
multiple orgasmic explosions in time...
you come to overstand
that i am no quitter, and wonder just how

i put that arch in your back...gazing
out of your window, awaiting my
return...not able to discern
the truth from the eye of the beholder...
hopeful emotions, closely held,
define moments of enclosure...clothed in carnal garments,
writhing with anticipation...
there exists no substitute for this
imposing beast
to whom you have been imprisoned...
who has made you see the light...caused
you to lose your inhibition...
who is this culprit, the cause of that glimmer?
made you believe in the unseen
infinite...left to your
own devices, this outercourse motivates dependence...
the return, patiently awaited for...
hopin' to further explore
your bio-rhythms...

civilizing mission

a man on an island, removed from himself,
no place in his world for him...
savage nature proclaimed,
reasons to be slain run the gamut of
civilization's justification...his darkness
goes against the light...
the light he brings may ignite a war...
more welts upon his sore back, he can stand...
they cannot stand by
while he becomes a man...of this world,
yet alien...the mayhem
may have been attributed to missionaries,
but they possessed a good
book...land taken in exchange...
processed trees for natural resources...
divorced from his way of life...
a life with no meaning before them...
saviors with behavior modification degrees...
sent to appease the kings and queens...
save the beast, teach him to say please...grant him
degrees in outsiderism...construct buildings
to house advanced student bodies...
payrolled into society, destined
to return...further the cause of his allegiance to massa...
natural disaster caused by heavy chains...
false knowledge reigns...painstakingly,
he plays the game of life...a grafted knife
inserted with care...
with hopes that st. nickel-less will always be there...

woolgather

saw you in a dream
my body began to vibrate
as our distance became non-existent
mental barriers broken
embarked on a journey
to meet in the outer regions
of our universe
hovering above the clouds
embraced by our essence   .
filtering the negative
as we floated beyond
the reach of doubt
drawing upon the internal
manifestation
of the life energy
to create reality
one mind
our time
took no notice
of the ground
beneath
our meeting extended
beyond the stars
to the place
we came to know only as
our own...
I awakened
to find no physical presence,
but still felt right
at home

sound subjugation

my energy is stored in silence...
   revealed to the page through
contemplation,
   i cease to regurgitate...
creatively self-determined,
   i aspire to innovate...
whispering souls speak volumes,
   symbols poured between tree bark etches
leaving permanent marks...
imperfect thoughts...
potential slow becomes kinetic flow,
   as cerebral synapses decongest...
articulate sounds manifest
   much to the dismay of my detractors...
perplexed and appalled by my vernacular,
   previously guarded, restricted by
reticence...
   faculty of reason cultivated
in the place where energy is stored,
   outside influence ignored
to the detriment of naysayers,
   conquest of the noise complete...

bill of pale

i pay no mind to trivial matters,
already make daily payments on the thoughts i gather...
with high percentage rates
on public debates...painful truth,
the creditor no man can escape...whether morally bankrupt
or spiritually challenged, still not enough capital
to reconcile negative balance...
virtual silence on real issues,
giving incorrect change...build a deficit
of brain power, a plethora of tame, uninterested herds,
futures dangling from a thread...
on loan from back home,
but they got all up in your head...now, my greatest challenge
is to settle up the books...
i add and subtract, ever mindful of the crooks
who stole land,
stole people, now they've stolen away...
under the cover of my darkness, proving that
white crime pays...

unsaved

faced with feelings of being inadequate,
i become the subject
which has no predicate...
punctuate with a period,
while questions remain...
going through changes, while
remaining the same...
who is to blame, but me,
for lack of growth...unreconciled
reality, my mind has been soaked
in the flames of destruction,
fanned by capitalist beneficiary...
they came cloaked as missionary
with hidden daggers...now i'm sent
to penitentiary after assault on carpetbaggers...
while braggers may boast of material wealth...
on any coast, i make the most,
despite lack of material health...
a shelved science project, proven
indestructible by man...a tax deductible,
proven slave hand...i go into labor, no chance
i will be born...nine months later,
still torn by the thorns engulfing my brain...
never been sane since my name was changed...
since i became three parts of a five part harmony...
patriotic enough to join a national Army,
and fight for demagoguery...laced
with lingo of democracy...my rise and fall
chained to calls of reveille...receive medals of honor

for being a good bondman...
life spent on a system designed
to harm my brethren...on many levels,
then, i have yet to be seen...invisible martyr,
yet to be redeemed...

water rise

going off the shallow end, yet in too deep...
try to keep my head above my feet...defeat is no option
for a man of my stature...natural cause of death the only
mentionable answer...a cancer to my community, heart
disease
for loved ones...trust neither,
trust none, except those with
trust funds for allocation to my cause...project walls
fill with names of victims,
fallen prey
who did not pray to be kept...many mothers
wept while many others slept on my abilities...trigger
the onslaught of psychosis...atrocious
diagnosis for the future...held by a hypnotic neurosis...
brain cells contain waves—held hostage...unable to escape
the pain of having my brain accosted,
inflicted, malnourished,
with misinformation served...on the verge of distinction as a
separate religion, with no savior...
no prophet to pattern my behavior...after the pain,
the profit begins...the doctrine of sin legitimizes the plates
i drop in...and, now i am good,
made a payment on my soul...death toll got me across the
bridge,
now living on the edge...
but i did not know the ledge was below my head,
and that is why i keep bumping it on the ceiling...revealing a
new truth, with god's name to back it...appealing to new
youth, as old lies attack it...attracted to shiny things, so i

take time to shine...
influenced by the gods, so they call me divine—knight
in shining armor, blessed by the sun, moon, stars...celestial
being,
meaning i have traveled distances
beyond all comprehensive study...delayed in my delivery of
this message—yet, still able to return to my essence...

natural causes

how can i not love the heavenly
body, dreams of soft
kisses placed strategically...not missing
your spotlight...ignite
like a cave, filled with my stick of
dynamite...body blows
up, as your back forms the half moon...
illusions of doom,
out of control, our souls connect like
artistic dots, or zodiac
hearts...each playing our parts,
as we begin to dig in...guilty as men
and women who sin,
together so beautifully—an unruly
force to be reckoned...at
my beckon; your call out to the gods,
begging for mercy...
mercy me, and oh my how wet you've
grown...better to receive
me—as i give my all to you, with
nothing more than love
for that heavenly body...
a heavenly party, and i provide favors
for you to savor...tongue
tickled navel to float your boat...
and French chocolate
kisses, directed toward spots missed in
the bombardment...
with no argument for or against

these sweet treats...glorious
freaks of nature perform feats beyond the
average imagination—
and, baby i can't wait to see that
heavenly body...

rotation and revolution

twice tonight the caring moon
broke the dark code...infiltrated my humble abode
amongst the stars...made waves
as the subplot sickened,
heart pace quickened by way of elation...
destiny fulfilled over conversation...a taste,
i received, mutual mind affection
relieved me of inhibition...on condition of anonymity,
given the remedy,
a modern rendition of an ancient play...
initiation dance advance the plot...
cosmic body set forth to
retrieve celestial downpour...down for
crown jewels, hood rules and ornaments...
hell bent and heavenly sent to free me...

soul elixir

there's something about the way
your words
curve through my nerve system...
unnerving in the
sense that i was born with
no rhythm...immediately seek the wisdom
of your words, your
example...configured for freedom,
though wandering with no aim—
controlled by word champions...
but you provide the saving grace, soothing
anguish with no weapon...
granting access to heaven—daily
conceived in your essence...
i wake from my slumber, and fill pages
with my blood...
raised from a hood, designed to construct
mass awakening...while
migratory animals try to destroy
my faith in them...
no hate for them, for in your words
i find only peace...direct
evidence increase my spiritual knowledge of the
beast.........

invisible man vision

i see apartment buildings,
open space...
retail chains, giving open chase
to the tender note with the old man's face...
enslaved men
who stay with an open case...of beer,
or litigation versus the state
for crimes committed while fitted with outer mind states...
sheer lunacy
how fluidly the universe flows...
sheer ignorance,
how the average mind is controlled...
sheer delight for the exploiters whose capital grows...
divine intervention, when
everyone knows of educational philosophy
from which atrocities flow...
education, redefined as regurgitated notes...
historical quotes promoting blind progressivism,
purposely out of context
to skew our vision of the future...
fruits of our labor have become forbidden...
highlights of the decay
leaving bodies bullet-ridden...
how fitting for those who claim to be supreme
to use destruction
as their reigning theme...
displaying true colors in the eyes of green,
showing true intentions
with elaborate schemes...detection of techniques

requires senses to be keen...
while they swerve and eject,
i'm eluding and fleeing...
from the grips of those who
question my being...
proceed through this jungle, all eye seeing...

congregation complexities

feeling out of sorts...
feeling like a sport, cause i am being played
short at six feet...
five inch pinch of reality
cause casualties in killing fields...
cheap thrills enthrall the poor...
give them more to feed on...
woman to beat on when it gets too hot...
police get their chase on,
take their best shot...a nigga gets dropped,
and public opinion, not...
this is the nature of a controlled flock...
stop,
look,
listen,
mention,
pay attention...
dissension in the ranks will take brains out of detention...
indecision becomes more costly
as we attempt to move forward...
up over the hill,
toward green pastures...
white gowns, with halos for caps...
consume whatever scraps i can scrape up...
take up
too much time to wake up in the morning...
running late to self-debate,
cause i don't know how to think straight...
push weight cakes in the name of survival...

rival clans battle over interpretation of bibles...
pilgrims
never held liable for destructive behavior...
Native population
must have had no Savior...
mass removal through murder and disease,
imperialist pursuits disguise
democracies...
root of all evil the source
which divides the suffering masses,
those who have been
cast aside...as the element of ,
time takes a toll on
the toil,
creating urgent matters before return to the soil...

diaspo-tragic

sleepless nights lead dreary days of musing...
losing my self
within the context of hyphenation...
conduct studies with hyper patience,
instruct students in basic transportation...
point A to Z,
three hundred sixty degree mind...
timepiece designed to decipher the beast nature...
climb virtual mountains
to reach peeks...paper gods provide
weak motivation to poverty stricken...
slim pickings in prosperity's midst
sickens, drives the point home...
from home, driven thousands of miles away...
thrown to wolves in shepherd clothing...
thousands in debt to pay...
public opinion sway
uncompelling to bottom feeders...prior deaths dissuade
potential civil rights leaders...
descendant black people breeders now want us to abort,
with reduction in criminals given as reason for this retort...
a flagrant disregard for the conditions criminals created...
short memory abated response to those hated,
unwanted,
undesirable,
unfulfilled dreamers...
dark continent partitioned by unrelenting schemers...
concurrent with destruction of black self-esteem,
construction of Declarations,

hypocritical themes...well versed,
though it seems poised to burst at the seams...
institutionalized malice for dark human beings...

she

good love,
bad times in lost worlds,
lost pearls passed down
through generations...
embrace the love education
which comes forth
from the queen...
unknowingly redeemed in her presence,
her grasp of my essence
fulfills me...answers my question,
bestows many lessons upon...
no less than the right wrong will rectify
this song in the key
of life, love, lust,
family built on trust in the signs...
connected minds perfected
when in unison...
unit formed, two becomes
one...and only she controls the keys
to my emotions...pours it on
in slow motion potion...
middle of the ocean, and unaware of
surroundings...astounding
ability to speak profound things
about our future
in eternity...love,
a certainty between
the queen and me...

new territory

your body is a garden of splendor...
a vast array of treasures,
ripened by purity—seasoned and awaiting
my next move...
a sigh of relief is exhaled,
as the work of angels is unveiled...
my eyes feast upon your
glory...your smile lights the room,
leaving an even pace far
behind in my heart—startled by utter beauty,
i become out of sorts,
as the fluid of life fills the gateway
to physical bliss...
oh, what will become of me once i am
free to investigate the potential
of your fiery cavern...
a ravenous appetite takes hold, once
unleashed, i am a bold
explorer of one—the
unfathomable wonders of god...

Part Three

So, how are we tomorrow
will be one of the most difficult times,
since the last time I saw your face
on the T.V. screen scenery was a beautiful sunrise
and set down at the podium
to speak fluently into the crowd got loud and clear
over and out dead and gone even
though I blew my horn, he still ran out in front of my car.

burdened path

slavery, an oppressed point of view
whose reality is based on the other...
submerged in a mis-educated sea
of visions, blurred by an unnatural
psychology of life and death...
self-destruction the main function
of the caucasian superiority assumption...
no matter how much we study this
conception,
the revelation brings forth no change
in the relation...
a death-filled struggle to obtain equal
opportunity to be white, and set it off
on the right...
the lighter you are, the less fight...
the darker, the harder...
not attemptin' to be a martyr,
only hopin' to be awakened before my life is
taken...
strivin' for leader, not follower...
intense internal battles inhabit the shallow
caverns of my mind...
a pilgrimage through meaningless tunnels,
in search of that which is divine...
attempt to escape created fate, consistently
ignoring the signs...
stay on the run from reality until
i run out of time...
time, the supreme master,
watch it go by without seeing it...
a life in God's image,   ,
watch it go by without being it...

desired

chocolate reply to my sweet tooth cravings,
saving every taste moment,
receiving rave reviews,
unlock the caged muse who goes by the phrase,
beautiful,
dutiful in my attention to all details,
sweet smells emanate,
orchestrate a coup of my keen senses,
defenseless in her midst,
recipient of her gifts
upon sight, useless to fight the revealing truth,
dark knight returned to roots,
fertile soil perception nourish the fruit,
body sings
the growth hormone song,
perfectly balanced,
blatantly challenge the reigning theme,
undeniable reverence for this Afrikan queen,
unseen characteristics clash,
dash hopes of deconstruction,
resumption of rulership to complete the cipher,
assumption of her throne,
what impurities aspire...

goddess moon

speaker of my words,
thinker of my thoughts,
substance of my dreams,
you reveal, to me, the essence
of life, and deliver me into
flowing streams...
going between dark and light
knowing the king will make
wrong right...dedicated to the endless fight,
you relieve me of concern,
for my heart burns the midnight oil,
awaiting your return...holding firm
to the rapture,
able to discern, my heart, long ago,
captured by, entangled in the web
of your purity...
surely,
this is the meant to be me...
sent to be with me...
heaven sent, opposing the
hell bent...divine intent of the goddess
Amira...

unexcused absence

monuments of nothingness
under construction...psychological dysfunction
justified...interrupted notion of equal access,
as i regress...strive for the unobtainable
instead...live in the red
just trying to stay fed, and keep a roof up over my head...
walking,
half-dead upon the landscape...
monetary bait dangled before my eyes...
never a surprise
when i choose the life of lies...
exception to the rule
for poor eyes to feast upon...false images
unleashed on the population...
no time for wasting on knowledge,
truth...
need s.tandardized a.ccess t.est scores for proof...
pro-assimilationist verification...
high marks grab invites to participation in prosperity
with no equality...
legitimized ideology from espoused theory...
un-rested,
weary,
weak,
tired...expired,
with only a legacy of denial to leave...
bereaved remnants left behind...
perceived distance from the past, so never rewind
or reply, with no hope to recoup...

free labor market economy regroup
to solidify tom's loyalty to a mystery...
god standing right before me...
phantom history,
legibly construed...literacy subdued
by the crude art of soul subjugation...
facing time for facing the nation...

misguided

intellectual harassment
the climax of my downward spiral
into a virtual muck created
within my psyche
    the mind molestation
    perpetrated by the soul-less ones
    enticing the vultures of the universe
    they trick me with time constraints
and give my life a dead line, knowing
full well that i should live forever
but my race for riches consumes me
reaching for empty promises of fulfillment
my ignorance chains me to man-made deliverance
without being concerned with true judgment
    a public figure, ordained and maintained
    epitomize the modern cultural controls
    distinguished in the child's eyes
historic in nature, yet still indulge in what is unnatural...

drug of choice/
ameriklan addict

these caucaine producers/users
be gettin' on my nerves...negativity,
death,
destruction, the only purpose they serve...
murderous, imperialists a cut above
all others...just look at,
see how they have raped my mother...
abusers,
high off the White substance,
devoid of melanin protection...they divided
her into sections for each of them to devour...
caucaine gives them super
inhuman powers
to deliver decisive blows...
and anything goes, despite what they espouse...
arouse suspicion within the crowd
when they smell of it, loud...
foul stench, monkey wrench any plans,
or semblance of peace...
false history feeds the beast nature...
love haters,
with an infinite supply, it seems...
crushing "i have a" dreams with elaborate schemes
to produce more of this drug
for generations to come...earth scum,
and jealous, rebellious ungodly one...
getting high on themselves,
forever in outer space...got my brothers
and sisters hooked after just one taste...

now we chase the caucaine,
always in need of a fix...
co-dependents,
remnants of a bad mix...
six feet under, above ground zombies roam...
speaking of the Resurrection,
in need of their own...
mental pictures,
caucaine scriptures,
hallucinogenic poison envy...
at school, even the teachers be trying to inject me...
selling lies for tuition,
getting permission slips signed...
so we can take trips to ancient
caucaine shrines...

fun damn mental

slave with a freestyle technique...
speak to the free
dumb...shun ties that bind my mental dexterity...
elevate through multiple
moments of clarity...thought the disparity could hold me
back,
down...member of the lost-found
nation of unknown to our selves...rebel yells and pumped
fists spark
thought revolutions...rebel solution does
not consist of inclusion...ruled by the illusion of equal access...
murdered Luther killed dream,
unfulfilled,
no signs of progress...civil unrest expose
the nature of the beast...confined to his belly,
devoured portions of the feast...
increase,
intense indigestion of ignorance...
lack of intellectual vigilance stalls my preeminence...
fill out applications
to be considered indigent...fulfill proclamations
denying my relevance...
elegant miniatures accent vanity chests,
represent my becoming without coming correct...
respect the empire
whose designs were my own...steady decline,
still fail to seek answers at home...
roam aimless, but not painless,
defeated,

destitute...destruction of these seeds
began with pulling out the roots...
nullifying the truth...
glorifying the noose...
same tune, different flute in the orchestra of my demise...
look through the prism,
same-ism wearing a different disguise—
appearances become clearer as i become of the wise...
change the angle of approach,
instrumental in my rise

oppressive duality

bell hooks in me,
remind of my propensity for
sex-ism...sex rhythm
given by my oppressor...created in
the supremacist image...master/slave
lineage inhibits...tendency
to express limits on freedom rides...
freedmen hide behind
the law, and join up...ticking modern
overseer, poised to self-destruct...in
need of deconstruction, de-massa-fication...
cleanse my mind, enhance
divine qualifications...strive for
true-to-life representation of manhood...whether in da 'hood
boyz, to mend the
'hood, boys must become men...i
stood, floored by
my own shortcomings...short
running essay put my innerisms on
display...injured rhythm, the
price i convey to my seed...failure to
heed the call, self-
victimization proceeds forward...ruled
by the coward i
strive to emulate,
make efforts to wake from this slumber in time...
thorough,
chattelbred from the finest...war crimes
committed left me custom split...

ahead in affliction, firm
in conviction against systematic inequality on race basis...
forced traditions inhabit bodies,
within i find traces...

blank pages

the blank pages of my book offer illusions of freedom
as i write them
i read them, wishing that
i could be the script that i write
non-melodramatic protagonist
cracking the case of the civilized fiasco
modern hero in disguise (masked marauder, uncovering eyes)
wise words of my predecessors
weapons of mass reduction to the numbers of the chained
triumphant story of the ages
fill the pages
progress in chapters
fulfill the dreams of main characters
the King
and i break barriers
more blank pages to fill
attainable illusion becomes surreal
confusion becomes creation in relation to the page
diffuse destructive forces
as i engage
make use of ancient tools
resume the story
hostilities rise in the region between the lines
blessed, by the Divine with more
blank pages

Printed in the United States
48162LVS00005B/692